SURVIVE! is published by
Stone Arch Books
A Capstone Imprint
1710 Roe Crest Drive
North Mankato, Minnesota 56003
www.mycapstone.com

Cataloging-in-Publication Data is available at the Library of
Congress website.
ISBN: 978-1-4965-2554-3 (library binding)
ISBN: 978-1-4965-2560-4 (paperback)
ISBN: 978-1-4965-2564-2 (eBook)

Designer: Hilary Wacholz
Design Elements: Shutterstock: Brothers Good, frikota, In-Finity,
Thomas Bethge, vladis.studio, zelimirz

Summary: Jeff and his best friend Keith are ice fishing in the
middle of Big Lake. It's been hours without a bite, but they're
still having a blast . . . until the storm of the decade closes in.
Soon, the entire landscape is buried in three feet of snow and
the snowfall shows no sign of stopping. With their heaters low
on power, Jeff and Keith are forced to make their way home
through the whipping wind, low visibility, and the ominous
crackling of ice beneath their feet.

Printed in China.
007500LEOS16

BLIZZARD

A TALE OF SNOW-BLIND SURVIVAL

> **BY THOMAS KINGSLEY TROUPE**

> **ILLUSTRATED BY KIRBI FAGAN**

SURVIVE!

STONE ARCH BOOKS
a capstone imprint

TABLE OF CONTENTS

CHAPTER 1

BOXED UP

Most of the people Jeff Ramis knew hated winter. They complained about the cold, the driving conditions, and shoveling their driveways. They hated wearing thicker clothes, warm hats, and puffy gloves. All winter long, people wished for spring and warmer temperatures.

Jeff, however, happened to love winter. And while he wasn't much of a skier and had long ago outgrown his red plastic sled, Jeff found something he loved even more: ice fishing.

The funny thing was, Jeff didn't fish much in the summer. It just didn't interest him. But he did like being out in the middle of a frozen lake with a friend or two, huddled over a hole in the ice, waiting for the familiar twitch on his fishing line.

Ice fishing was just more fun for Jeff. A challenge. A way to make the long winter more enjoyable.

So, on a Saturday night in early February, Jeff was sitting in his dad's old ice shack in the middle of Big Lake with his best friend Keith Willis. A few hours in, he hadn't gotten any bites — but Jeff refused to go home empty-handed. Keith wasn't a big fan of fishing, but he'd come along anyway claiming he had nothing else to do. He'd yet to bait his hook.

"You should decorate this shack," Keith said, looking around. "Hang up some posters or something."

Jeff glanced around the shack. Old pictures of his dad and his buddies were tacked to the walls. They held their catches high in the winter sun, smiling through ice-encrusted beards. He didn't think he

could take his dad's pictures down. They were sacred in a way.

"Nah," Jeff said with a smirk. "But if you ever catch something, I'll take your picture and put it next to the other photos."

Keith grunted. "Yeah, right," he said. "Like that'll happen."

But it worked: Keith actually baited his line and dropped it into the dark hole next to Jeff's. They each jigged their lines in silence for a while.

After a few minutes, Jeff grabbed a large spoon and scooped the slush out of the hole to keep it from freezing over.

"Check out that old radio," Keith said. "We should find some music to listen to."

"Sure," Jeff said. "Let's scare away the fish."

Keith stood up and picked up the radio. "You're kidding, right?" he asked. "I don't think fish have ears anyway. Let's see if this old thing works."

Jeff shrugged. "Fine," he said. "Give it here."

As Keith handed the radio over, a knock came from the shack's door. Jeff reached over and pushed the door open. His dad poked his head in.

"How's it going, men?" Jeff's dad asked.

"Slow night," Jeff said.

He stepped in, pulling the door closed behind him. A few flakes of snow speckled his dad's reddish beard. His wool hat was pulled down over his ears.

"Catch anything?" Dad asked, nodding at the hole.

"Maybe a cold," Keith said with a smile.

Jeff shook his head. It was plenty warm in the shack, but Keith could never resist a chance to crack a joke.

"We're not catching anything in our shack, either," Dad said. "Hey, that old radio still work?"

"Not sure," Jeff said. He flicked the power button and adjusted the volume.

The light at the top of the old radio didn't light up. He popped the back compartment open. The batteries inside were faded with age.

"Batteries are probably dead," Keith said.

Jeff rolled his eyes. "Yeah."

"What're those, 'C' batteries?" Dad asked, reaching for the radio.

Jeff handed it over. He jigged his line while Dad examined the radio. The fish needed something exciting to chase, after all.

Dad set down the radio. "I'm taking the truck into town real quick for some burgers," he said. It's not even six yet, and Randy and Skip are already whining about being hungry. Amateurs."

Jeff smiled. His dad had fished with the same two friends pretty much forever. They usually flipped a coin to see who had to run into town when they got hungry. His dad's friends didn't seem to enjoy fishing all that much, but they sure seemed to enjoy hanging around together — and eating burgers.

"You must've lost the coin toss," Jeff said.

"Smart kid," Dad said. "Anyway, I'll grab some food for you two fish-heads — and some batteries."

"That works," Jeff said. "Thanks."

"But keep it down, would you?" Dad said as he closed the door. "No singing or air-guitaring or whatever you kids do these days. You'll scare all the fish away."

Jeff gave Keith a look. They both smiled.

"You can't scare fish in an empty lake, Mr. Ramis," Keith said.

"You just gotta be smarter than the fish, Keith," Jeff's dad said.

"Oooh," Keith groaned. "Ouch."

"See you soon, guys."

With a smile and a nod, Dad was gone.

CHAPTER 2

WHITE OUT

The wind whistled across Big Lake, making the little ice shack creak. The gusts made ghost-like noises in the cracks and seams.

"Dad's new shack isn't this noisy," Jeff said. It felt a little colder in the shack, so he turned the heater up a little. The generator outside chugged along, struggling to power the lights and heat.

"That wind better not pull a big bad wolf on us," Keith muttered. He fidgeted around with a flashlight he'd found in the backpack they'd brought.

"What do you mean?" Jeff asked.

"You know," Keith said. "That one story about the wolf and the three little bears eating pudding. How he blew their house down?"

Jeff chuckled. "Dude, you're mixed up. It's about three *pigs*, and they weren't eating pudding."

"Yeah, whatever," Keith said, laughing. "It's so cold, I think my brain is numb."

Jeff laughed. He pulled his line up from the hole. "I wonder what's taking my dad so long," he said.

"No kidding," Keith said. "We need that radio. Want me to rap or something?"

"Please don't," Jeff said. He stood up. "Maybe Randy and Skip have heard from him."

Jeff pushed on the warped wooden door. It didn't budge. Something was blocking it from the other side. He pushed again. The door moved a little.

"What's going on?" Keith asked.

"The door," Jeff said.

He pushed again.

Jeff's foot slipped on the ice and he fell, slamming most of his weight against the door in the process. It opened a few inches and snow sifted in from the darkness outside.

Keith set his rod down and crawled over. Once Jeff was back on his feet, they both pushed. Together they managed to open the door enough to see the winter wonderland outside.

The snow was much higher than it had been even forty minutes ago when Jeff's dad left. It whipped around the giant lake. Jeff couldn't see far. Snow dunes had formed from the wind. The sky was filled with white flakes.

"This is nuts," Keith said. "It's a full-on blizzard!"

The lake was so dark and full of snow that Jeff couldn't even see his dad's nicer, newer ice shack through the storm. They weren't going to be able to see anything — not until it stopped snowing.

"Think your dad got caught in this storm?" Keith asked.

"I don't know," Jeff said. "His truck can drive through just about anything, but no one knew we were getting *this* much snow."

"Yeah," Keith said. "It's too bad it didn't work — the radio would've warned us."

Jeff nodded and kicked out as much snow as he could before trying to close the door. Keith crawled on his knees and shoved out some snow as well.

"We'll end up buried at this rate," Jeff said.

"As much as I hate to say it," Keith said. "It's probably best to just stay here for now."

Jeff knew Keith was right. They'd be foolish to try to find their way back. Besides, Jeff didn't even know if his dad was back or not. With his luck, they'd get to the edge of the lake where the truck had been parked only to discover it was still gone.

"Yeah, let's wait it out," Jeff said. He sat back down on the small bench. The hole in the middle of the floor was already icing over again.

A moment later, the lights went out.

CHAPTER 3

COLD ESCAPE

"What happened?" Keith asked in the darkness.

"The generator died," Jeff said softly.

Jeff couldn't see a thing in the complete darkness. As he felt his way over to the other side of the shack, his boot caught on something and he fell hard on his arms.

"What're you doing?" Keith asked.

"Trying to find that flashlight," Jeff said. He picked himself up, rubbing his elbow.

A moment later, there came a click!

Keith's illuminated face stared back at Jeff. Then Keith made his eyes cross and he frowned like a monster from an old movie.

"Quit messing around," Jeff said. "If that generator doesn't start, we're in big trouble."

"What? Why?" Keith asked.

"No generator, no power," Jeff said. He scanned the small enclosure with his flashlight. He spotted the backpack and a small shovel against the wall. "And no power means no heat."

"No heat, no good," Keith said with a sigh. "Yeah, let's get that generator going."

Jeff grabbed the shovel and pulled Keith's line out of the water.

"That should be good," Jeff said. "We can leave everything else in here for now."

The two of them forced the door open again. Even more snow had fallen since they'd last had it open. Jeff was no meteorologist, but they'd gotten at least three feet of snow so far. Maybe more.

"This is nuts," Jeff said. "Look at all of it."

Keith pulled his zipper up higher so that the collar surrounded his neck. "I hate winter," he said.

The two of them trudged through the snow. To Jeff it felt like they were wading through cold, white sand. It took a surprising amount of energy to move even twenty steps. Thirty-two slow steps later, they were behind the icehouse.

Keith shoved some of the snow off the generator. "It's buried," he said. "No wonder it conked out."

Jeff whistled. He handed the flashlight to Keith. He dropped down to his knees and started clearing away the snow with the shovel.

Keith trained the light over Jeff to help. "Can you find it?"

"Yeah," Jeff said after a few more shovelfuls. "Getting close now."

Afraid he'd damage the old generator, Jeff set the shovel aside and used his hands to remove the remaining snow.

After a few armfuls of snow, he felt the ridges on the top of the machine. It was completely cold after getting buried in the blizzard's onslaught.

Jeff cleared the remaining snow from around the generator until he found the ripcord.

"Start it up," Keith said, shivering. "Hurry, it's freezing out here."

Jeff pulled the cord and heard the generator sputter uselessly. He pulled it again. And again. The engine refused to turn over.

"It's not happening," Jeff said. "Time for plan B."

CHAPTER 4

GET LOST

Jeff knew he needed to move fast. It was cold, they had no power, and the snow was continuing to fall. At the rate it was coming, they'd end up buried like the generator in thirty minutes, tops. And, eerily, one word kept popping into Jeff's mind . . .

. . . Frostbite.

Jeff's dad had lectured him once on not wearing a hat while ice fishing. When Jeff got home, he looked up "frostbite" on the Internet. He immediately wished he hadn't.

The photos of people who'd suffered severe frostbite had purple and blue skin. Sometimes their fingers had turned coal-black. In the worst cases, the victims had to have toes or fingers removed. Or noses.

It was the stuff of horror movies. Jeff loved the winter, but he also knew that severe cold and wind combined were nothing to mess with.

Jeff pulled his hat down over his ears a little more. "Let's get over to the other fishing shack," he said. "Maybe Randy or Skip can call my dad. Either way, at least we'll keep warm."

"Makes sense," Keith said with a nod. "Lead the way, man."

Jeff grabbed the shovel. Using his ice shack as a landmark, he headed in the direction he thought was south. His dad and his buddies liked to try out different spots on the lake, so it wasn't always in the same place. But when they'd arrived earlier that evening, their shack was set up about one hundred yards south from Jeff and Keith's.

It would be easy enough to see during the day, but it was almost impossible in a blizzard at night.

Keith raised the flashlight. The beam of light was littered with giant white flakes, scurrying to find their places in the growing pile.

"Do you know where we're going?" Keith asked.

"It's this way, we can't miss it," Jeff said. "We'll hear those guys telling dumb jokes any second now."

"Good," Keith said. "I can't see anything."

After trudging forward for a few minutes, Jeff glanced behind them. He saw their footsteps trail off into a wall of white, but he couldn't see where they began. There was no sign of their abandoned ice shack, either.

Do you honestly know if you're heading in the right direction? Jeff thought.

When they'd walked another ten minutes, a sinking feeling crept into Jeff's stomach. "We should have found them by now," he said. "Maybe we went the wrong way."

Keith swung the flashlight back and forth, as if searching for the shack on his own. "No way!" he shouted. "That's impossible!"

Jeff knew his friend was likely as worried as he was. They were completely lost in a blizzard in the middle of a giant, frozen lake. *At least Keith is nice enough not to point out this was my idea,* Jeff thought.

Keith's snow pants swished as he forged ahead through the waist-high snow.

"Wait," Jeff shouted. "Let's trace our steps back to the ice house. Maybe my dad is back."

He heard Keith stop. The beam of the flashlight aimed back at him. A moment later, he saw his friend through the white flakes. "Okay," Keith said.

They turned and followed their footsteps back toward the shack — only to stop after a short distance.

Their tracks were gone.

CHAPTER 5

NO HELP

Icy gusts blew across the lake, stinging the skin on their exposed faces. Jeff put his snowy gloves to his face, covered his cheeks and eyes, and exhaled hot air to make a mini face furnace.

"Does that help?" Keith asked.

"A little," Jeff said behind his gloves. "For a few seconds, anyway. If we keep moving in a straight line, we'll eventually reach the edge of the lake. From there, hopefully we can find a house or a car, or something."

Keith sighed. "Sounds good."

They trudged along in silence. Jeff secretly hoped they weren't traversing the diameter of the lake, which would make the journey nearly three miles.

In other words, Jeff thought, *dead meat.*

"Hello!" Keith shouted, nearly making Jeff jump out of his snow pants. "Can anyone hear me?!"

It was hard to hear anything over the blowing wind, but Jeff heard Keith's voice echo. It wasn't a bad idea. It'd keep them occupied and active, at least. So they both shouted into the white-specked darkness, hoping for any sort of response.

After ten minutes of yelling, no response came.

Jeff was starting to lose his sense of time — and more importantly, his sense of direction. He wondered if Randy, Skip, and his dad were out looking for them. Using his gloved hand to shield some of the snow from his eyes, he scanned the horizon. He couldn't see any flashlight beams other than Keith's.

"Jeff!" Keith shouted. For a moment, Jeff let himself hope that the two of them were saved.

He followed Keith's light. At the end of the beam was the corner of an ice fishing house.

"Is that it?" Keith asked. "Is that your dad's icehouse?!"

Jeff didn't have to look at it long to determine that it wasn't. The ice house they'd found was a pre-fabricated store-bought shed made of metal. Jeff's dad liked to build his sheds by hand, "the way real fishermen did."

Even so, the two of them moved closer. There were no lights or signs of life near the shack. Jeff reached the door in the hopes they could use it as a temporary shelter — only to discover the door was padlocked.

"Can we break in?" Keith suggested.

"No tools," Jeff said with a shrug. "Besides, I don't see a generator. We'd still freeze our faces off."

Keith went silent, and Jeff understood why: If they didn't find some help or shelter real soon, they wouldn't survive.

"We have to keep moving," Jeff said. "And find some place warm. Or a way to call for help."

Keith didn't say anything, but trudged onward. Jeff followed.

After what seemed like another hundred yards, Keith cried out again. "Hey, I see something. It's a sign, I think!"

Jeff looked up to see Keith running ahead, plowing through the snow.

"Wait!" Jeff shouted, realizing what the sign was. A second later he heard a loud *CRACK!*

Following Keith's trail, Jeff saw Keith's tracks end at the edge of a hole in the ice. The flashlight was lying in the snow, but Keith was gone.

CHAPTER 6

BREAKTHROUGH

Jeff stopped dead in his tracks. He knew without looking that the sign read: THIN ICE.

Jeff fought back the urge to panic. He needed to act fast. He peered at the hole in the water, but he couldn't see Keith. That meant his friend was somewhere under the ice.

"Keith!" Jeff shouted. He wasn't sure if his friend could hear him, but it was worth a shot. When he didn't hear or see any sign, he used the small shovel to check the strength of the ice next to his feet. He tapped the surface a few times and took careful steps toward the flashlight.

The ice creaked a bit as he neared the light. Using the shovel, he dragged the flashlight across the snow to within arm's reach.

Jeff aimed the beam at the icy hole, hoping that Keith would be able to see the light and use it as a beacon to find his way out. He held his breath, listening carefully.

Nothing.

Then, below his feet, the ice shook slightly.

He's pounding on the ice! Jeff realized.

Jeff cleared away some of the snow with the shovel. The ice was too thick where he was standing to see Keith, but he moved the snow anyway to clear a path toward the hole. He illuminated the makeshift path he'd created.

"C'mon, Keith," Jeff said. "Follow the light."

The wind died down, making it eerily quiet. Jeff traced the beam of light along the ice path he'd made. Then he pointed the beam into the hole itself for a moment before starting to trace again.

The black opening in the ice began to get as slushy as their ice fishing hole.

"Hurry, Keith!" Jeff shouted at the top of his lungs. "Get to the hole!"

A moment later, a wet, gloved hand rose through the water, quickly followed by Keith's pale face.

"Keith!" Jeff shouted. His voice echoed around the lake.

"G-get me out of here!" Keith screamed.

Jeff lay flat on his stomach to spread his weight out evenly along the ice. Using his gloved hands and shovel, he pulled himself closer to the hole.

The ice beneath him started to crack, but It didn't matter. Jeff had to keep moving.

"Grab the shovel," Jeff said, watching his friend flail around in the open water. "And stay still! You'll need your energy!"

Gasping, Keith reached for the shovel.

"Get your fingers in the handle!" Jeff cried.

If Keith could grip the top of the handle, he could at least keep his friend above water.

"I can't reach it," Keith sputtered, cold water spraying from his mouth.

Jeff inched closer, certain that the ice would crack any second and dump him in, too. When it didn't, he scooted forward a bit more. Keith reached out and locked his finger into the handle.

"Got it," he said.

"Now swim out!" Jeff cried. "Kick your legs and swim toward me. Grab a thicker part of the ice!"

"I can't see . . . how thick . . . it is," Keith said between shudders. "Just p-pull me out!"

Jeff hauled his friend closer to the edge. "C'mon!" Jeff shouted. "Get as much of your body onto the ice as you can!"

Keith nodded. Jeff saw his friend's breaths come in quick, ragged gasps. As he kicked and rowed his free arm, Jeff pulled. Keith climbed out so his ribs were resting on the ice.

"Pull!" Keith shouted.

"Kick your legs!" Jeff cried.

Jeff tugged and screamed and closed his eyes. He heard his voice carry through the blinding white expanse around them. He kept tugging.

Finally, he heard a splash. He opened his eyes to see his friend fall face-first into the snow.

CHAPTER 7

SOAKED

Keith was silent. Jeff wasn't sure for how long —
it felt like minutes, but it probably was only seconds.
In that space of time, Jeff was convinced Keith had
died. He couldn't see any breaths coming from his
mouth, and he wasn't moving.

Then he heard a loud cough come from his
friend's mouth. "Jeff?" Keith whispered. "I'm cold,
man. I'm freezing from the inside out."

Keith curled himself into a ball. The flashlight
glinted off of his water-soaked winter clothes.

Now what do I do? Jeff thought. He took a deep breath. Cold air filled his lungs. *First things first, I have to get us off the thin ice.*

Jeff slid back a little. He didn't want to be too close to Keith or the ice would surely give way. "Can you roll over?" he asked.

"What?" Keith whispered.

"Roll away from the hole," Jeff said. "Toward me."

Keith groaned. Slowly, carefully, he rolled away from the icy hole. Jeff crawled backward, inching his way through the snow, farther and farther from the thin ice.

"I think we're safe here," Jeff said. He stood up and carefully pulled Keith to his feet.

"I'm freezing to death," Keith whispered. Jeff could hear his friend's teeth clacking together. "What are we gonna do? I don't want to be a Popsicle . . ."

"We need to get you somewhere warm," Jeff said.

Jeff had no idea where that might be, though. Moving forward wasn't an option anymore, and he didn't dare head back the way they'd just come.

"My jacket and snow pants are too heavy," Keith cried, his breath ragged and choppy. "They must weigh like two hundred pounds."

"Let's wring them out," Jeff said. "Quick, pull that stuff off."

Jeff helped Keith out of his outer layers of clothing. Together, they twisted the soaked fabric to squeeze out as much water as possible. They did the same with his hat and when they were done, Keith put it back on.

"I'd pay a million bucks for a bonfire," Keith said as he zipped up his still slightly wet coat. Jeff watched Keith's entire body shiver.

Jeff picked up the shovel and the flashlight. "We're gonna walk that way now," Jeff said, using the shovel to point in a direction parallel with the thin ice. "I'll test the ice with the shovel before every few steps."

Keith had his arms wrapped around himself. He nodded. Jeff could only imagine how Keith felt right then.

I don't know how much time we've got, Jeff thought, taking his first few cautious steps forward. *If someone doesn't find us soon . . .*

They moved slowly, testing the ice in front of them and listening for tell-tale cracks. They continued on, slowly making their way across the great, white expanse.

CHAPTER 8

BRIGHT LIGHT

Jeff and Keith continued through the blinding snow and wind, still unable to see any sort of life outside of their small range of vision. Jeff was tired, cold, and ready to give up. Seeing how much Keith was struggling, though, gave him the strength to keep moving.

"We have to get you warmed up," Jeff said a few minutes later. "The next icehouse I see, I'm going to see if I can set it on fire."

Keith nodded. "You . . . criminal."

Jeff chuckled. His friend still had his sense of humor, at least.

They pressed on.

Jeff looked up to the sky. Staring up through the falling snow and clouds, he couldn't see a single star — just billions and billions of snowflakes falling softly onto everything in sight.

Keith groaned. "I have to stop. My body feels like it's shutting down."

"Mine too," Jeff said. He grabbed his friend by the arm. "But we have to keep moving. If we rest, we might never get up . . ."

Keith shuddered. "Okay," he said. "And hey, man. I never thanked you."

"For what? Asking you to come out ice fishing?" Jeff said. "Yeah, really turned out well for us, huh?"

Keith made a sound more like coughing than laughter. "No," he said with a wan smile. "Not that. Thanks for saving me. If you hadn't shined that light on the hole, I would've drowned."

"No problem," Jeff said. "I'm just glad I didn't have to jump in after you."

"Me too," Keith said. Then he dropped to his knees. The snow was up around his waist now, and getting deeper by the second. "Sorry, but I have to rest."

Jeff watched his friend's eyes slowly close in the waning beam of his flashlight. The batteries were likely dying. In moments they'd be in total darkness.

Jeff slowly waved the now-flickering flashlight back and forth over his head. The odds of anyone seeing it in the whiteout were slim, but he had to try. His friend was running out of time.

"C'mon, Keith," Jeff urged. "Get up. Get up, man."

The flashlight died. Jeff looked around, waiting for his eyes to adjust to the darkness. Suddenly he saw two single beams of light bearing down on them.

Great, Jeff thought. *Now I'm delirious.*

He slumped down next to his friend. He could barely hear Keith breathing. Jeff blinked his eyes as hard as he could. When he opened them, the beams of light were still visible.

Jeff struggled to his feet and waddled over to the light. A moment later, the beams enveloped him and Keith. After a moment, he realized what they were.

"Headlights!" he croaked.

Seconds later, his dad's pickup truck was there igniting the snow around them in a wide swath of light. Jeff tugged at Keith as his dad hopped out of the truck.

CHAPTER 9

WARMTH

Together, Jeff and his dad got Keith into the backseat. The heat felt amazing against his skin.

"I got to the ice shack and saw it was empty," his dad explained, driving through the whipping snow. "I couldn't see where you'd headed."

Jeff explained how they'd ended up lost and wet. He smelled the hamburgers in the front seat and his mouth began to water.

Keith groaned. "We're going to make it," Jeff said. "Just hang tight."

"Burger," Keith said weakly.

"That's right," Jeff said, feeling his body begin to thaw. "You want one?"

"Yeah. To heat up my face," Keith said.

They both laughed.

The truck raced across the lake, heading for the hospital. Jeff stared out the windshield, recalling the cold and the darkness. He shivered despite his warmth.

For the first time in his life, Jeff wished for summer.

WINTER SURVIVAL NEEDS

Getting caught in severe winter weather is no joke. Proper preparation is key to survival. These items will help to ensure your safety in a blizzard.

Clothing: Staying warm and dry is vital. Thermal socks, waterproof clothing, and thick boots will go a long way to shield you from the icy elements.

Fluids: Staying hydrated is crucial, especially during long storms. It may seem obvious, but the places one would typically find water will likely be frozen in severe winter weather.

Fire: Matches or a lighter can provide heat in case of power outages. Some lighters will not work unless they are warm, so matches might be a safer choice — unless they get wet. Ideally, matches should be sealed in a waterproof container.

First Aid Kit: The kit should include the basics — but also a fully charged cellular phone and some emergency rations.

Compass: Whiteouts make it nearly impossible to figure out where you're headed. A compass will point you in the right direction.

Flashlight: Power outages are common in severe weather. Just make sure you have the correct type of batteries!

Batteries: Power outages are common during blizzards and other types of severe winter weather. Access to a generator is ideal.

Shelter & Food: The best way to be prepared for a blizzard is to STAY INSIDE! A warm and safe place with plenty of canned goods will all but guarantee you live to tell the tale.

ABOUT THE AUTHOR

Thomas Kingsley Troupe Thomas Kingsley Troupe has written more than thirty children's books. His book *Legend of the Werewolf* (Picture Window Books, 2011) received a bronze medal for the Moonbeam Children's Book Award. Thomas lives in Woodbury, Minnesota, with his wife and two boys.

ABOUT THE ILLUSTRATOR

Kirbi Fagan is a vintage-inspired artist living in the Detroit, Michigan, area. She is an award-winning illustrator who specializes in creating art for young readers. Her work is known for magical themes, vintage textures, bright colors, and powerful characterization. She received her bachelor's degree in Illustration from Kendall College of Art and Design. Kirbi lives by two words: "Spread joy." She is known to say, "I'm in it with my whole heart." When not illustrating, Kirbi enjoys writing stories, spending time with her family, and rollerblading with her dog, Sophie.

GLOSSARY

amateurs (AM-uh-choors)—people who are poor at doing something due to a lack of experience

eerily (EER-uh-lee)—strange and mysterious

expanse (ek-SPANSS)—a large and flat open area

frostbite (FRAWST-bite)—a condition in which part of your body freezes or almost freezes

generator (JEN-uh-ray-ter)—a machine that produces electricity

glinted (GLIN-tid)—shined in small bright flashes

jigged (JIGD)—made quick and sudden movements

onslaught (AWN-slawt)—a violent attack

traversing (truh-VERSS-ing)—moving across an area

WRITING PROMPTS

1. Make a list of things Jeff and Keith could have done to be better prepared for the blizzard. What would've made their situation safer or easier?

2. Choose another type of natural disaster and write a story about it. What are you doing when the disaster strikes? How do you manage to survive? Write a short story about your own survival.

3. Rewrite one of the chapters in this book from Keith's perspective. In what ways might he see things differently from Jeff?

DISCUSSION QUESTIONS

1. What would you have done differently if you were in Jeff and Keith's situation? Why?

2. What surprised you about what Keith and Jeff experienced during the blizzard? What aspects of severe winter weather did you already know about?

3. As a group, come up with a list of words to describe a blizzard, like cold, frigid, and chilly. Try to come up with fifteen words.